7852

Kitchen, t
Gorilla/Ch illa

$11.32
~~$13.89~~

DATE DUE

		1998
FEB 1 3 1999	NOV 3 0 1999	2 9 07 998
MAY 0 4 1999	FEB 1 5 2000	98
MAY 0 4 1999	FEB 1 9 2000	4 1998
JUN 1 5 1999	MAR 1 5 2001	98
JUL 27 1999	MAY 2 5 2001	
AUG 1 7 1999	AUG 2 1 2001	
OCT 1 3 1999	MAR 1 6 2002	
MAY 0 8 2004	JUN 1 5 2004	
JAN 2 5 2005	OCT 1 5 2005	
AUG 0 9 2005	MAR 1 1 2006	
AUG 2 6 2006	APR 0 6 2006	
FE 2 0 07	APR 2 0 2006	

HIGHSMITH #45231

E
Kit 852

OC 0 4 07

Gorilla/Chinchilla

AND · OTHER · ANIMAL · RHYMES ·

Bert Kitchen

DIAL BOOKS · NEW YORK

"What's your game?" says Kinkajou
  To the parrot, upside down.
"Don't you know," says Cockatoo,
"I'm famous as a clown.
  So come on, let's play peekaboo
  Before you climb back down."

"Oops-a-daisy," grunts the Hog,
  As Frog hops overhead.
"That splashy, sprightly, springy Frog
  Makes me feel as heavy as lead.
  Who wants to chase him around the bog?
  I think I'll nap instead."

In nature you'll agree

Most creatures do their best.

The Beaver gnaws the tree.

The Weaver builds its nest.

The Beaver cannot see

Why he'll be called a pest.

The Tortoise looks back in dismay.

She feels her foothold shift.

The "stepping stone" begins to sway.

Her back foot starts to lift.

And when the Porpoise swims away

She's sure to come adrift.

"Can you do this?" says Pelican,
His large beak gaping wide.
"Who needs to," says the Toucan
As he turns round goggle-eyed.
"It only means that you can
Hold a lot more air inside."

7852

"Who's throwing that soil without any care?
    Ah ha, it's you, dear Mole.
    Next time you dig you should beware.
    I could get hurt," says Vole.
"Make sure that I'm not standing there
    Next time you dig your hole."

It's curious how contrary
Some animals remain.
For though the Cassowary
Is clearly far from plain,
The dull, proud Dromedary
Still treats her with disdain.

The Grison stands erect.

He can't believe his eyes.

What's caused this shock effect?

This paralyzed surprise?

The Bison we suspect

And its overwhelming size.

The Salamander gulps in fear

As Zander seeks its prey.

It isn't safe to enter here

Till Zander swims away.

Best wait until the coast is clear

Or bathe another day.

One day the Hippopotamus,

While trudging so wearily,

Looked down to see just what it was

Moving more easily.

He spotted the Duck-billed Platypus

Swimming by effortlessly.

Whoa there! thinks the Beagle,

I'd better turn around.

If I play fetch with that Eagle,

He'll fetch me right off the ground.

He looks mighty fierce and regal

While I'm a mere pup of a hound.

The Iguana suns on a stone;

The Jacana stalks nearby.

Each thinks he's all alone

Beneath a peaceful, clear blue sky.

But soon there'll be a different tone

When bird meets lizard's eye.

"What's up there in the sky?
    Please tell me, old friend Seal.
    No matter how I try,
    I can't see it," says the Teal.
"If something's caught your eye,
    I wonder if it's real."

When Chipmunk pops up for fresh air,

He sniffs foul air instead.

His whiskers twitch, his nostrils flair:

That smell can't be misread.

For Skunk is there outside the lair

With the odor we all dread.

The sight of a Gorilla

Fills most men with alarm.

He looks like a killer;

He's sure to cause harm.

But see this frail Chinchilla

Nestled in his arm.

The moose shown on the title page is pictured with a snow goose, an Arctic wild goose.
Some of the less familiar animals featured in this book include:

CHINCHILLA · A furry South American rodent

KINKAJOU · A tree-dwelling South and Central American raccoon

COCKATOO · An Australian parrot

HOG · The hog featured is a warthog, a wild pig of Africa

WEAVER · A finchlike bird noted for its elaborate nests

TOUCAN · A fruit-eating bird of South and Central America

PELICAN · A web-footed bird with a large pouched bill

VOLE · A rodent related to the American field mouse

CASSOWARY · A flightless bird of Australia and New Guinea

DROMEDARY · A one-humped camel

GRISON · A weasel-like South and Central American mammal

BISON · The American buffalo and certain related species

ZANDER · A central European perch

SALAMANDER · A long-tailed amphibian

PLATYPUS · An egg-laying Australian mammal

IGUANA · A large lizard of South and Central America and the southwestern United States

JACANA · A long-toed, long-legged wading bird

TEAL · A small, short-necked wild duck

For Mum and Jim

Published by Dial Books · A Division of Penguin Books USA Inc.
375 Hudson Street · New York, New York 10014
Published simultaneously in Canada by Fitzhenry & Whiteside Limited, Toronto
Copyright © 1990 by Bert Kitchen · All rights reserved
Design by Atha Tehon
Printed in Hong Kong by South China Printing Company (1988) Limited
First Edition
E
1 3 5 7 9 10 8 6 4 2

Library of Congress Cataloging in Publication Data
Kitchen, Bert.
Gorilla/Chinchilla / Bert Kitchen.
p. cm.
Summary: Rhymed text and illustrations describe a variety of animals
whose names rhyme but who are of very different habits and appearance.
ISBN 0-8037-0770-3—ISBN 0-8037-0771-1 (lib. bdg.)
[1. Animals—Fiction. 2. Stories in rhyme.] I. Title.
PZ8.3.K65625Go 1990 [E]—dc20 89-16851 CIP AC

The paintings were prepared using watercolor, gouache, and colored pencils.
They were then color-separated and reproduced in full color.